ATTACK OF THE LEGION OF DOOM!

SCRIPT WRITTEN BY JIM KRIEG
ADAPTED BY J. E. BRIGHT

SCHOLASTIC INC.

ISBN 978-0-545-86799-3

10 9 8 7 6 5 4 3 2 1   16 17 18 19 20

Printed in the U.S.A.   40
First printing 2016

CHAPTER 1: A NEW LEADER

ON A DARK STREET IN METROPOLIS, the intergalactic villain Darkseid stood triumphantly on a hunk of rubble. Superman, Wonder Woman, Green Lantern, Hawkman, and The Flash lay on the ground, unconscious. Batman kneeled before Darkseid.

"And so the Justice League falls!" the criminal crowed. His eyes glowed, shooting deadly beams at Batman.

Cyborg leaped in front of Batman, blocking Darkseid's attack with an energy shield. The villain's beams ricocheted, blasting a wall. Bricks toppled on Darkseid.

"Booyah!" Cyborg cheered. "Surrender now, Dorkseid!" He threw up his arms. "World's Best Cyborg!" he hollered. "Disco time!" As a glittering disco ball appeared overhead, the Justice League jumped to their feet and danced.

"I put the boogie in borg!" yelled Cyborg as he wiggled to the music.

Batman patted Cyborg's shoulder. "You saved my life," he said. "Impressive. We should hang out more. I've got a pool table back at the Batcave—"

R-R-R-RING!

Cyborg woke up. He was suspended in his charging station in the Hall of Justice. "*Ah*, dang.

I overslept!" he cried. "I'm going to be late for the meeting . . . again!" Cyborg scrambled out of his room, ran through the corridors of the Hall of Justice, and skidded into the Great Room. Superman, Batman, Wonder Woman, The Flash, and Green Lantern watched him enter.

"You're late, Cyborg," growled Batman.

"*Uh*, hi, everybody," Cyborg said sheepishly as he took a seat.

"Vic," asked Green Lantern, "don't you have an atomic clock built into you?"

"Think nothing of it, young Cyborg," Superman interrupted. "We started without you."

Superman raised his hand for attention. "It's Election Day," he said. "We'll be voting for a new hero to lead the Justice League." Behind Superman, holograms of his campaign posters appeared. "Please, everyone, vote with your heart."

The teammates pressed buttons on their consoles to vote. Batman peered up at the holographic display showing the results. "It looks like a tie, since Superman and I undoubtedly voted for ourselves."

Superman's eyes widened. "That never occurred to me," he said. "I voted for you."

"And the winner is . . . Batman!" announced Cyborg. "All right, Dark Knight!" He raised his palm for a high five, which Batman ignored.

The Trouble Alert flashed, clanging its alarm. The Justice League rushed over to the monitors.

"A robbery at the Metropolis First National Bank," said Wonder Woman.

The Flash tilted his head at Batman. "What's the word, chief?"

"The word," replied Batman, "is go."

The Justice League raced into their high-tech ship, the *Javelin*, and soared toward downtown Metropolis. As they arrived, a villain in a yellow outfit burst out of the bank's front doors to find the police waiting for him. The criminal giggled.

"Freeze!" a cop hollered. "Hold it right there, Joker!"

"I'm not the Joker!" the villain shouted back. "I'm the Trickster. Totally different."

Superman called, "Ah, our old friend, the Trickster."

"Finally!" replied the Trickster. "He gets me."

Superman leaned close in to his teammates so they could hear him whisper. "I know he isn't really our friend. I was being ironic." Then he flew between the villain and the police. "Come quietly, Trickster!"

The Trickster held up a canister. "You either let me go," he threatened, "or we're going to have a smelly situation on our hands."

"I got this!" shouted Cyborg. He shot a sonic blast at the Trickster, which spun the canister into the air. "And now to dispose of it." He took aim.

"Wait!" warned Batman. Cyborg fired his laser cannon. The canister exploded, releasing a noxious green gas, which drifted into the city.

"I did it!" cheered Cyborg. "Booyah!" Then he got a whiff of the gas. "Ew! What's that smell?"

Citizens and the police glared angrily at Cyborg as they held their noses.

"Glad I'm not in his shoes," said Green Lantern. He created a giant fan with his power ring, and blew away some of the stinky gas.

"I was trying to tell you, Cyborg," Batman said, "that was a stink bomb. Now this whole section of the city stinks."

"Not to mention you guys," added The Flash.

The Trickster giggled as Superman dragged him off to jail. "Looks like I got the last laugh!"

Cyborg squirmed and said, "Oops?"

CHAPTER 2: AMBUSH AT AREA 52

CYBORG TRIED to get his mind off his embarrassment with what happened with the Trickster by tinkering with the technology of the Hall of Justice. He twisted a glowing bolt with a wrench. Electricity shot up his arm and sizzled his circuits. Cyborg fell backward, twitching.

A robot he had built peered down at him worriedly. "Have Cyborg's functions terminated?"

"No, Cy-bot," groaned Cyborg, "I was working on some new upgrades for the Hall. I'm distracted. I made a big, stinky mess today, and I'm not so sure the others want me around."

With a sigh, Cyborg climbed to his feet. He strode out of the equipment room. Cyborg walked to the Great Hall, where he found his teammates. "*Whoa!*" he gasped. "What's going on?"

"Our former costumes were ruined with a permanent stench," Batman answered. "It compromised our effectiveness as crime fighters."

Cyborg looked down at his boots. "Right," he whispered, "because it's my fault your old ones got all stinky."

"Nonsense," said Wonder Woman. "We all needed a change. Why don't we come up with something new for you, too?"

“We can’t,” replied Batman. “Cyborg doesn’t wear clothes.”

A loud alarm echoed in the Great Hall and red lights flashed.

“The Trouble Alert!” announced Superman. An angry military man with a white moustache appeared on screen.

“Justice League,” the man said, “I am General Lane, commanding officer of Area 52, a top-secret government installation. We are under attack from person or persons unknown. But it’s probably . . . alien.”

“You say that like it’s a bad thing, general,” replied Superman.

“Just get over here,” insisted General Lane, “and take—”

The image fuzzed out in snowy static. "Let's go," said The Flash. "I can feel myself growing older just standing here."

Superman put his hand on The Flash's shoulder. "Not so fast. Batman is our elected leader. This is his call."

The members of the Justice League waited for Batman's decision.

"Prepare the *Javelin* for launch," said Batman.

In their supersonic craft, the Justice League soared toward Area 52. "Look alive, team," ordered Batman as the *Javelin* began to descend. "We've entered Area 52 airspace."

"Ooh," said Cyborg, "a spooky, top-secret government compound. How'd you even know where to find it?"

Batman narrowed his eyes. "I'm—"

"Batman," Cyborg finished. "Right. Gotcha."

The *Javelin* landed on the tarmac of Area 52. The Justice League stepped out into the eerie silent stillness of the base.

"It's quiet," said Batman. "Too quiet."

"Truck!" screamed Cyborg. He pointed up at the sky, where a huge sixteen-wheeler big rig tumbled toward them.

Green Lantern created a force-field dome that saved the team from getting crushed. When the dust cleared, the Justice League was amazed to see a group of super-villains standing on the tarmac. Captain Cold, Gorilla Grodd, Cheetah, and Black Manta struck a dramatic pose.

Hovering above them was Sinestro. "Welcome to your defeat, Justice League," he said, creating giant yellow words behind him with his power ring. "Defeat at the hands of . . . the Legion of Doom!"

"Copyright and trademark," added Captain Cold.

CHAPTER 3: BATTLE ON THE BASE

"DESTROY THEM," Sinestro ordered the Legion of Doom.

"Justice League, move out," commanded Batman."

"You heard our captain," cried Superman, swooping into the air. "Let's move!"

While Green Lantern battled Captain Cold, Cheetah pounced at Wonder Woman. "The Legion of Doom will have your heads!" Cheetah screeched.

Wonder Woman sidestepped, and grabbed Cheetah's tail. "Tails, you lose," said Wonder Woman. She spun Cheetah around in a circle.

Nearby, Gorilla Grodd bounded toward Superman. Before he got close, Superman exhaled sharply, blowing the muscular ape through the wall of an airplane hangar.

Superman flew in the hole, scanning the inside of the dark warehouse. "It's no use trying to hide from me!"

"Who's hiding?" growled Grodd. Brilliant lights flashed as Grodd rose up atop a spinning flying saucer. "I'm just getting a feel for my new ride." He shot energy rays at Superman, nailing him in the chest.

"Hey!" cried Superman. "I felt that!" He dodged around the rays, zooming through the hangar.

Outside, Sinestro flew above Cyborg, who ran across the tarmac. "School's in session, youngster," yelled Sinestro, trying to hit Cyborg with a giant yellow sledgehammer.

Cyborg shot his arm cannons at Sinestro as he ran. "Well, here's my homework!"

Sinestro avoided Cyborg's attack, and took careful aim. He blasted Cyborg with an energy beam, knocking him into a pile of crates. "Class dismissed."

"Hey, Sinestro!" The Flash hollered behind him, racing closer at super-speed. "Here comes your worst nightmare."

"My worst nightmare involves public speaking in my underwear," replied Sinestro. "You're not even close." He created a speeding train and aimed it at The Flash.

The Flash rushed along the side of the train, zipping toward Sinestro. "All aboard the haymaker express," he exclaimed as he hit Sinestro hard. "Ha, ticket punched!"

Sinestro spun around, dizzy, but he cleared his head quickly. "Take this, you parasitic pinball," he sneered, creating bumpers and paddles around The Flash.

The Flash got caught in the pinball game, bouncing around. "Whoa!" he cried, falling down.

"Full tilt, loser," said Sinestro. He lowered himself to where Cyborg was alone. "Now to finish off the half-man." He created another gigantic hammer to smash Cyborg.

Cyborg protected himself under a small energy dome. With every smash of Sinestro's hammer, the dome held, but the ground around it cracked.

"So, robot man," Sinestro teased, "is that all you can do? Sit there while the real men do the work?"

As Batman and Black Manta battled nearby, Wonder Woman stopped spinning Cheetah and let her go. Cheetah tumbled through the air, and grabbed ahold of Gorilla Grodd's head as he passed by on his flying saucer. She clung to his face.

"You frustrating feline," gasped Grodd. "I can't see!" The saucer tilted and dipped.

Taking advantage of Grodd's distraction, Superman landed on the edge of the UFO, running on it to make it spin wildly.

The saucer whizzed out of control, smashing to the ground. Grodd and Cheetah skidded across the tarmac and ended up in a heap.

With a sonic boom, Lex Luthor appeared in a cosmic tunnel next to them. He had a big cylindrical container with him. "Legion of Doom!" Lex called. "Mission accomplished. Let us make our victorious retreat!"

CHAPTER 4: STOLEN ALIEN

"WHAT'S LEX GOT THERE?" asked Superman.

" Nothing good," replied Batman.

The inter-dimensional tunnel retracted and vanished, taking Lex Luthor and the cylinder with it.

Having heard Lex's call to retreat, Sinestro started to fly away, but Cyborg fired a grappling hook and caught the villain's ankle. Sinestro created a buzz saw and cut Cyborg's cord. Then he turned the saw into a gigantic dustpan. "Here's a pop quiz," he told Cyborg, swatting him with the pan. "You failed."

Sinestro swooped over the tarmac, scooping up his fallen teammates with the dustpan. "Once again, it's up to me to clean up after lesser people's messes." He carried the other members of the Legion of Doom over to Black Manta's ship.

Superman soared after them, but before he could grab the ship, it launched, vanishing at warp speed.

General Lane stormed over to the group. "You let them get away!"

"So, what? The only thing they got was a giant can of soda or something," said Green Lantern.

The general held up a file with a picture of the cylinder on the front. "It was an alien!" he yelled. "And you let it slip through your fingers because of your incompetence." He narrowed his eyes at Superman. "How do I know all you aliens aren't in cahoots?"

"Hey!" argued The Flash. "Superman isn't an alien! He's a . . . oh, yeah, I guess he kind of is."

Superman hovered above General Lane. "The real question is," he said, "why are you incarcerating aliens?"

"*Ah*, well . . . " stammered the general. "I'm not the one being questioned here! Now, if you'll excuse me, I've got government property to locate." General Lane strode away.

Superman looked worried. "Surely our government isn't arresting extraterrestrials."

"Based on my analysis of his behavior," replied Batman, "it's more likely that General Lane has greatly exceeded his authority."

Cyborg hung his head, looking sad.

"Why the long face, Cyborg?" asked Superman. "You held your own against a formidable opponent. Good job!"

"Good job?" cried Cyborg. "If it wasn't for me we could have stopped them."

"You're still the youngest member of this team," Wonder Woman said gently. "Cut yourself some slack."

"The question is," said Batman, "what happens next time we meet?"

CHAPTER 5: MELTDOWN

IN THE BASEMENT of the Hall of Justice, Cyborg and Cy-bot added cables and specialized bricks to the technology of the headquarters. Cyborg touched the wrong circuit. Bolts of energy zapped him and Cy-bot. They fell onto their backs. "It's no use," said Cyborg, sitting up. "Not even my hobby can clear my mind. I need some advice."

"Can't get up," moaned Cy-bot. "Help."

Cyborg strode out of the basement. He found Wonder Woman on the roof watching the sunset.

"Listen, Vic," said Wonder Woman, "you look at your recent battles and see mistakes. That's just your perception, but it's certainly not my perception of you." Cyborg smiled slightly. "You're a young hero," Wonder Woman continued. "You have to trust your instincts and give yourself time to grow."

Cyborg nodded. "So," he said, "you're saying I should really beef up my cybernetic components?"

"What?" blurted Wonder Woman. "No."

"Thanks, Wonder Woman!" cheered Cyborg. "That's exactly what I'll do!" He rushed off the roof. Moments later, he was welding in his workshop.

"I don't know why I didn't think of it before," he said as he attached an enormous cannon onto his shoulder with Cy-bot's help. "I've got to gear up! Booyah!"

With an array of new weapons, Cyborg strolled confidently through the corridors. He passed Batman on the way to the Great Hall. "What's up?" he asked.

Batman ignored him.

A few seconds later, Cyborg strode past Green Lantern. "How's it going, Hal?"

"I'm living the dream, Vic," Green Lantern replied.

Cyborg resumed walking toward the Great Hall.

Then he passed Batman again. "Batman," he said with a nod.

"Have a nice day," said Batman, walking on.

Cyborg whistled as he strolled. He stopped, and rushed back toward Batman. "This may sound strange," said Cyborg, "but I passed you twice, and I don't think—"

Batman glared. "Perhaps if you concentrated on being a super hero instead of butting into other people's business, you'd be a better Justice League member."

With a gulp, Cyborg backed off. "Sorry," he said, his feelings hurt. He hurried away. When Cyborg reached the Great Hall, Superman, Wonder Woman, and Batman were entering at the same time.

Cyborg gathered his courage and approached Batman. "Hey," he said, "maybe that was meant to be constructive criticism when I passed you just now, but—"

"I didn't say anything when you walked by," replied Batman. "You must be getting a double image in your cybernetic eye. Let me help." He smacked the side of Cyborg's head, causing his eyes to spin. "There," said Batman. "Better?"

The red lights and sirens of the Trouble Alert blared.

Cyborg rushed over the monitor. "It's that prototype Nuketron Reactor that just went online," he said. "The one that should provide a solution to the world's energy needs."

"By Hippolyta's hairnet," swore Wonder Woman. "It's in danger of a total meltdown."

"Let's go," said Batman.

The Justice League flew in the *Javelin* toward the Nuketron Reactor. As they got close, the heroes looked out the window at the building below. It was a giant dome in the center of the city. Red lights flashed around it as steam rose from cracks in the dome.

"Cyborg," asked Green Lantern, "how long before the energy core melts down?"

Cyborg peered down through his cybernetic eye. "This is strange," he reported. "My readouts don't detect anything wrong. Everything looks normal."

"Time for an oil change, Tin Man?" Green Lantern asked. "Look at that thing. That's about as normal as Batman smiling."

Batman faced his team. "Cyborg and I will secure the perimeter," he instructed. "Flash, you and Wonder Woman get the crew out of that inferno. Superman and Hal, you're both immune to the reactor's radiation. Stop the energy core from melting down . . . or else Metropolis becomes a lifeless radiation hot zone for the next 10,000 years."

"*Uh*, that's a pep talk?" asked Green Lantern.

"Let's do this, guys!" The Flash whizzed across the lot where workmen used a crane to hoist bricks. He zoomed in and grabbed them. "Don't worry, fellas! I'll have you out of danger in a flash!"

Cyborg and Batman hurried toward the plant. Cyborg blinked his robotic eye. "Batman," he warned, "I'm still reading everything is normal."

"We'll deal with your software glitches when we get back to the Hall," said Batman.

CHAPTER 6: CAMERA ONE/ CAMERA TWO

AS HE AND CYBORG reached the reactor, Batman activated his comlink. "Superman, Hal," he asked, "what do you see?"

On the other side of the site, Green Lantern soared above a damaged pipeline. "The coolant pump between the water supply and reactor core is toast," he reported. "No wonder it's overheating."

Superman swooped over the reactor's dome and scanned it with his X-ray vision. Inside, he saw a woman holding a video camera in the control room. It was Lois Lane! A violent rumble shook the reactor. A heavy piece of computer equipment fell off the wall, pinning Lois underneath. Superman blasted through the reactor wall, smashing his way through the building's layers.

Superman grabbed the equipment and tossed it aside. "There you go, Lois." Sirens blared, and Superman scanned the damaged core. Its coolant had dropped to dangerous levels. "Now let's get you out of here before—"

To Superman's surprise, she had vanished entirely. "Lois?"

An explosion rocked the reactor. Superman was blasted against a wall as the room glowed red-hot. He winced at the intense radioactive heat. "Batman," he reported, "the core temperature is hotter than the sun. We're in full meltdown!"

"You have to cool the core to a safer temperature long enough to get it out of the building," replied Batman.

"I'll do my best," said Superman. He inhaled deeply, then released his freeze breath.

Ice rippled over the core's sizzling surface. It cooled the core a little . . . but not enough to keep it from melting down.

Superman charged underneath the shielded core, and heaved it up on his shoulders. Together, he and Green Lantern pushed the core out through the top of the reactor, shoving it upward until they had left the Earth's atmosphere.

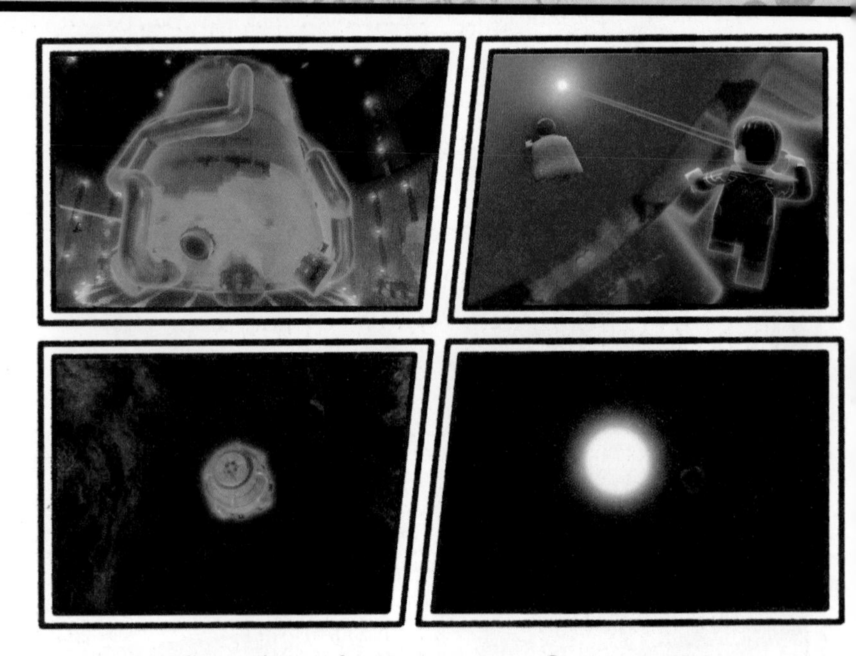

Up at the edge of outer space, Superman gathered his strength. “Hold steady and get ready,” he told Green Lantern. “Here . . . we . . . go!” Superman hurled the core away from the Earth. The core exploded halfway to the sun.

“Saved the day,” said Green Lantern. “Again!” He and Superman smiled at one another, and they headed back to Metropolis.

Down in the reactor, Cyborg reached the room where the core had been. He stared at the mess, first with his human eye. He saw the melted room that Superman and Green Lantern had dismantled. “Camera one,” said Cyborg.

Then Cyborg looked at the room with his robotic eye. "Camera two," he said. The only damage was from Superman's freeze breath and Green Lantern's ring. He looked at Batman. "Something's funny here," he explained. "And I mean funny messed up, not funny ha-ha. There was never anything wrong with the reactor."

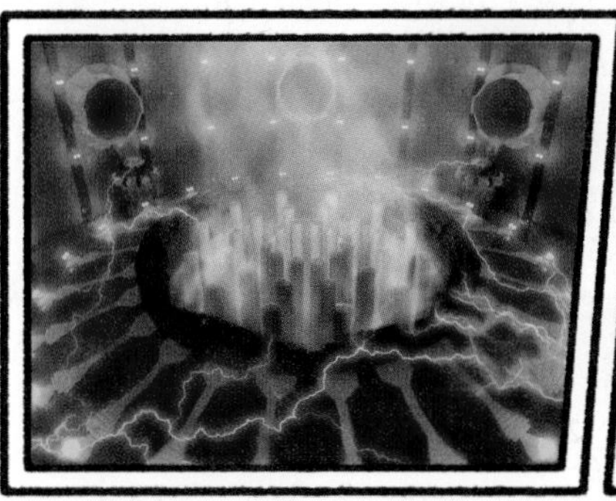

The Justice League gathered around Cyborg and Batman as Green Lantern and Superman returned to Earth. "I'm beginning to think you're right," said Batman, although he was facing in the other direction, staring at a large crowd of reporters, police officers and angry plant workers.

"Why did you destroy our power plant?" one man demanded.

Superman cleared his throat. "You may not have noticed your plant was experiencing. . ." He trailed off as he saw that the reactor looked completely different. "A meltdown?"

"Now it looks less melty," said The Flash.

Lois Lane rushed up to Superman with her camera. "You and the League have just destroyed a multibillion dollar power plant that could have made Metropolis a world leader in efficient energy production," she said. "What do you have to say for yourselves?"

"Lois?" exclaimed Superman. "You're okay."

"Okay?" shouted Lois. "I'm livid, like everyone else on Earth. What do you tell your critics who claim the Justice League has too much power?"

"*Whoa*," said Green Lantern. "What critics?"

"My daddy, for one," replied Lois.

General Lane stepped up beside Lois with a stern expression.

"He's your daddy?" Wonder Woman asked.

Cyborg scratched his head. "Who's your daddy?"

"I knew he was your daddy," said Batman.

"There was no meltdown," declared General Lane. "The reactor was working fine." He faced the crowd. "Do you see, people? We let superpowered goons run around unrestricted and this is the type of thing that is bound to happen. The so-called Justice League needs to pay for its crimes," the general continued. "They must be controlled before something worse takes their place."

"Down with the Justice League!" a workman yelled.

An angry woman added, "I used to like them but now I don't!"

Cyborg covered his human eye and peered at the mob. In the back was a green alien! He gasped and lowered his hand. The alien vanished.

"People, people," Superman said. "Don't panic. This has apparently been one big misunderstanding. The Justice League is all about responsibility. I'm sure that once we've explained everything, the World Court will happily find us—"

CHAPTER 7: BANISHED

"GUILTY AS CHARGED! For the charges of stink bombing Metropolis, attacking a government facility, and nearly causing a nuclear meltdown," General Lane read from the verdict, "the Justice League is banished from Planet Earth! Effective immediately!"

"All right," growled Batman, "this conspiracy has gone far enough. We have to get to the bottom of it." He started to slink offstage. "We're going dark. Off the grid. We'll work from the shadows to solve this mystery—"

"Nope," said Superman, grabbing Batman by his cape. "Not this time. The Justice League was formed to serve the governments of the world. They overrule your authority, Batman. If they want us gone, we go."

"Nice speech, alien," said General Lane. "Guards, get these heroes out of my sight."

Later that afternoon, the members of the Justice League packed up their belongings and loaded them into the *Javelin*. Then they launched out of the Hall of Justice roof, heading into outer space, leaving Earth behind.

Green Lantern sat next to Cyborg in the ship. Cyborg trembled robotically as they passed the moon. "Wipe away those tears, Cyborg," said Green Lantern. "It's a big galaxy. Stick with me and we'll have a blast. I know a planet inhabited by broken toasters. Maybe we'll find you a girlfriend."

Wonder Woman joined Superman in the cockpit. "I think you can let go of Batman now."

"Oh," said Superman, releasing him. "Sorry about that. But the law is the law."

Batman smoothed down his uniform. "We'll discuss your little mutiny later. Our job now is to gather evidence, prove we were framed, and then return to Earth."

"I'm afraid returning to Earth is not an option," sneered Sinestro.

The Justice League glanced up to see the yellow villain floating in space.

"I just came to give you a farewell gift," said Sinestro.

"I hope you kept the receipt," Green Lantern retorted.

The *Javelin* fired its weapons, but Sinestro created a yellow energy shield. He yawned as the beams bounced away.

"Keep firing!" insisted Green Lantern. "He'll have to keep up that shield and won't be able to attack."

"Think so?" asked Sinestro. He held up a tablet. "Meet my new best friend. It's called a Father Box."

He activated it, creating a huge, swirling tunnel disappearing into space. "Doesn't this just bowl you over? Prepare to be flushed to the other side of the galaxy!" Then Sinestro created a humongous plunger, and shoved the *Javelin* into the cosmic tube.

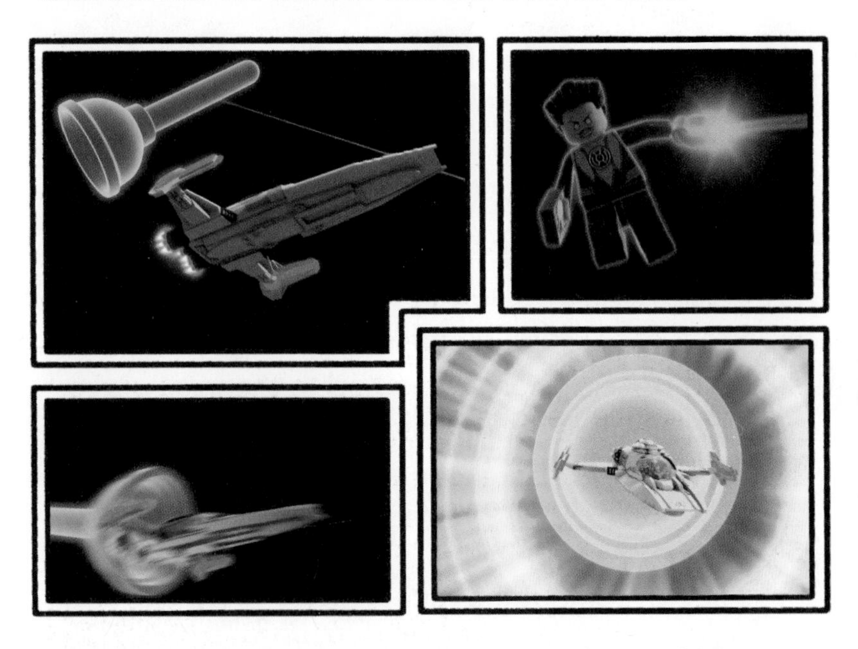

With a whooshing sound, the *Javelin* swirled through the portal.

"Oh, I get it," said The Flash. "Bowl! Flush! Like a toilet."

Then he and the Justice League screamed as they spun into another dimension.

CHAPTER 8: MARTIAN MIND CONTROL

THE JAVELIN SPAT OUT of the tunnel in the farthest reaches of the galaxy, beside a vast black hole. "We're caught in the pull!" Green Lantern yelled. "Everybody hang tight!"

Green Lantern exited the *Javelin*, and created a small spaceship around himself. His ship launched a strong tether, which connected to the front of the *Javelin*. The line snapped taut as Green Lantern tried to tow the Justice League to safety.

"I'm giving her all the willpower I've got, but I can't escape the black hole's gravity," Green Lantern reported. "At least we're not being sucked in anymore. You guys all right back there?"

"S'all right," muttered Cyborg. He fizzled with electricity and fell to pieces. Chunks of him slammed into the back wall.

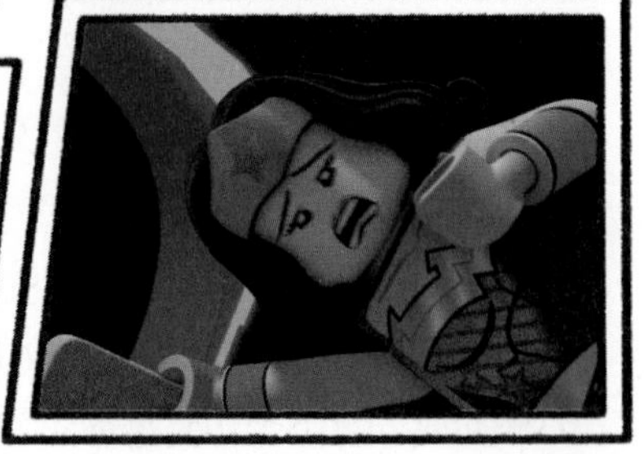

"Oh, poor friend," gasped Wonder Woman. "I shall sing the Themysciran Song of Dead Heroes for you!"

Batman held up his hand. "No need to sing. He's just a dummy."

"That doesn't matter," said Superman. "He was our friend!"

The Flash picked up Cyborg's head. "No, he means a real dummy," he explained, showing the team that the head actually belonged to Cy-bot. "He was acting weird ever since takeoff."

"Which leaves us with two questions," said

Batman. "How do we get out of this jam . . . and where is the real Cyborg?"

The real Cyborg was in the Hall of Justice. He was adjusting the electronics in a wall panel. "I hate to leave the guys in the lurch," he muttered, "but I know there is something fishy going on." He shook a monitor, and a strange device dropped onto the floor.

"A clue," said Cyborg, picking it up. "Some kind of weird alien technology. How'd this get here? Better check the security tapes."

Cyborg fast-forwarded through the camera footage, and spotted a strange alien wandering the halls. "Oh, I know you," he said. He checked his own camera's footage from the power plant.

"Aha!" crowed Cyborg. "That's the alien I saw. I knew he couldn't be some random green guy in red underwear. Now all I have to do is get this evidence out there and clear the Justice League."

"Clear them with whom?" asked Sinestro.

Cyborg whirled around to see the yellow villain floating in the Great Hall.

"Within a few hours," Sinestro said, "the Legion of Doom will have taken over the world. Only one member of the Justice League left . . . and it's the weakest one." He laughed. "I think you already know how this ends, don't you, half-man?"

Cyborg shot a sonic blast above Sinestro's head.

"You missed," said Sinestro.

Then a chunk of blasted ceiling toppled down on Sinestro, flattening him.

Cyborg rushed outside. "Got to keep moving," he gasped. "This evidence is more important than me getting payback."

"Go ahead, run!" shouted Sinestro. "It'll make your final defeat more enjoyable."

Cyborg leaped away from Sinestro's fire. He bounced across the gardens, and clambered up the side of the building to the roof.

Sinestro cornered him, but before he could deal a wallop, he stopped and looked worried. "What?" the villain gasped. "The Justice League? Alive! Impossible." He glared maniacally at invisible people around him.

The green alien materialized behind him. "Not impossible," he said, placing his hand on Sinestro's head, "for me."

Sinestro's eyes blanked out. "You are under my mental control," the alien said. The alien lowered him down to Cyborg.

"You're the shape-shifter who set us up," said Cyborg. "What did you do to him?"

"Martians like me have the ability to influence minds," the alien explained. "Organic minds. Unlike yours, Cyborg."

Cyborg nodded. "Everyone else saw the plant malfunctioning because you were making them see that," he realized. "But my cyber-organic brain is immune to your powers." Cyborg pointed his sonic cannon at the Martian. "I still don't trust you."

"Please," the alien said. "I am here to help."

"Like you helped the heroes of Earth get banished?" argued Cyborg.

The Martian hung his head. "I was tricked. Lex Luthor freed me. I let my thirst for vengeance cloud my judgment. Forgive me. Let me make this right."

"How?" Cyborg asked.

Again, the Martian placed his hand on Sinestro's head. Sinestro raised his power ring and activated the Father Box that created a galactic tunnel.

"All right, Sinestro," said the alien. "It's time to unflush the Justice League."

Sinestro laughed. "Flush. That's a good one."

The tunnel circled into another dimension.

In front of the black hole, Batman, in his spacesuit, pushed against a wing of the *Javelin*. Superman pushed on the other wing, while Wonder Woman heaved against the tail fin. In front, Green Lantern's ship pulled on the tether. The Flash sat inside, working the controls in the cockpit.

"Keep pushing!" Green Lantern insisted.

"The *Javelin* is a state-of-the-art spacecraft," Batman grumbled. "I never thought we'd have to get out and push." His eyes widened as a portal appeared in front of Green Lantern's ship.

"Athena's fallen arches!" shouted Wonder Woman. "Our way home! Everyone heave!"

Inch by inch, the *Javelin* shifted toward the portal. Seconds after they made it through, the tunnel swirled closed.

CHAPTER 9: DOOM IN METROPOLIS

BACK ON EARTH, the Justice League rushed into their headquarters. They saw on the monitors that the takeover of Metropolis by the Legion of Doom was already underway. The Hall of Doom floated over the city, raining down destruction on the buildings and citizens.

"Okay, here's the plan," said Batman. "Hal, you, The Flash, and Wonder Woman take out the Hall of Doom. Superman and I will stop Grodd and the forces on the ground."

"What about me?" asked Cyborg.

"I need you to stay in the Hall, Cyborg," replied Batman. "Hold down the fort, and also keep an eye on this Martian."

Cyborg bit his lip. "But I want to go with you."

Batman looked into Cyborg's eyes. "By going rogue, like I wanted to do, you saved us all. But now I need you to make sure Sinestro and the Martian stay put. Can you do that, soldier?"

Cyborg sighed. "Yes, sir."

A few minutes later, Grodd advanced along an avenue atop a tank as his mechanical monkeys rampaged. He pounded his chest. "Victory is ours!"

"Not quite," said Batman. The Dark Knight swung onto a ledge, armored in his Bat-Mech. "Don't worry, Grodd. You can have all the bananas you want in Blackgate Prison."

Gorilla Grodd pointed at Batman. "Destroy him!"

The tanks fired laser beams, but Superman swooped down, blocking them with his chest. The robot apes attacked, too, but in his suit, Batman handled them easily.

High above Metropolis, Green Lantern and Wonder Woman flew toward the sinister Hall of Doom.

Cheetah announced to Wonder Woman, "I've got a little surprise for you!" She fired laser beams.

Wonder Woman deflected the lasers with her silver bracelets.

"*Uh*," said Cheetah, "that wasn't the surprise. This is the surprise!" She launched tentacles out of the side of the Hall of Doom, which bound around Wonder Woman.

Wonder Woman flexed, bursting the tentacles apart.

"We're out of surprises," Cheetah told Lex Luthor inside. "How do we stop her?"

Lex Luthor made a fist. "By exploiting her one weakness," he answered "Her compassion! Launch missiles!" Two fiery missiles trailed out of the Hall of Doom, passing Wonder Woman on either side.

"You missed!" shouted Wonder Woman.

"Did I?" Lex replied.

Wonder Woman whirled around. The missiles hit the base of a skyscraper. The building teetered, and slowly fell toward an animal hospital.

"No!" screamed Wonder Woman. She zoomed toward the falling building at top speed. It had fallen too far for her to push it upright—all she could do was hold it in place.

Down below, Superman hurled tanks, smashing them. "You're less fun than a barrel of monkeys!" he shouted.

A green beam shot from the Hall of Doom. It hit Superman square in the back.

Superman screamed and flattened against the street. "No! Kryptonite . . ." he gasped.

Batman had challenged Gorilla Grodd in hand-to-hand combat when he saw Superman was in trouble. "Hold on!" he hollered. "I'm coming!"

Another beam fired down from the Hall of Doom, blasting Batman's armor into smithereens.

Grodd grabbed Batman and hoisted him into the air, laughing victoriously.

In the Hall of Justice, Cyborg and the Martian gaped at the destruction on the monitors.

The Martian shook his head. "The Hall of Doom was specifically designed to withstand your powers and exploit your weaknesses. It is only a matter of time before it defeats the entire Justice League."

"Not the entire League," replied Cyborg. "I have an idea!"

CHAPTER 10: HALL AGAINST HALL

CYBORG RAN TO A CONTROL PANEL and plugged wires from his arm into the ports. Lights flashed and the Hall of Justice trembled.

The Martian struggled to keep his balance. "What's happening?"

"I gave it an upgrade," Cyborg said. "It's my hobby! Three . . . two . . . one . . . hold on!"

The Hall of Justice shuddered. Rockets underneath it ignited. It rose into the sky.

"Let's show them we've got style!" cheered Cyborg. "Launch disco missiles!"

Dozens of rockets with glittering disco-ball warheads shot out of the Hall of Justice.

The missiles smashed into the Hall of Doom and exploded.

Down on the street, Superman punched Gorilla Grodd so hard that he flew backward, crushing a tank. Batman fell free and Superman helped him up.

"Good to know you've got my back when it counts," said Batman.

Superman smiled at the destruction overhead. "Looks like Cyborg had all our backs."

"He's going to make a great leader someday," added Batman.

The two flying battle stations shot everything they had at one another. Even during the Hall of Doom's merciless final assault, Cyborg was prepared. "Star shield, activate!"

The Legion's attack bounced harmlessly off the Justice League's force field.

Cyborg grinned. "I call this my in-your-face finale," he told the Martian. Then he launched hundreds of missiles with a picture of him smiling on each one.

This final assault blasted the Hall of Doom. It fell, smoking and exploding, toward an empty park below. It smashed into the grass, digging up dirt and rocks, until it skidded to a stop.

The Hall of Justice landed next to the disabled Hall of Doom.

The Martian and Cyborg raced out of the headquarters. Cheetah, Black Manta, Captain Cold, and Lex Luthor had survived, and were limping away on foot.

"You aren't going anywhere!" yelled Cyborg. He took aim.

The Martian put his hand on Cyborg's arm. "Please," he said. "Leave this to me." He soared toward the villains, who attacked him with their remaining strength.

But the Martian knocked out Cheetah, Captain Cold, and Black Manta.

"Looks like you always get your man," said Cyborg. "Like you're a . . . Martian Manhunter!"

"*Hmm* . . . I like it," said Martian Manhunter.

Of the Legion of Doom, only Lex Luthor remained standing. He faced Martian Manhunter. "If it wasn't for me," Lex said, "you'd still be held prisoner."

"For that I am grateful," said Martian Manhunter.

Lex smiled. "So you'll let me go?"

"Yes," Martian Manhunter replied. "But they may not."

The Justice League surrounded him, glaring at Lex.

Later, as the Legion of Doom was loaded onto special police transports, a crowd of citizens gathered to celebrate. "Hooray, Justice League!" they shouted.

"Sorry we exiled you!" one man yelled. "Our bad!"

"Thanks to you, Cyborg, the Earth is out of danger because you trusted your instincts," said Batman. He held out his hand. "Good job."

Grinning, Cyborg shook Batman's hand.

Superman and Wonder Woman flanked Martian Manhunter. "I'm sorry about the way this planet treated you when you arrived," said Superman, "but sometimes we're suspicious of something we haven't seen before."

Batman looked at his watch. "According to the bylaws of the League, I'm only leader for another . . . 37 seconds. Then it'll be time for another election."

"You've still got my vote, Bats," said Superman.

Batman nodded at Martian Manhunter. "My final act as leader is to offer a Justice League membership to our new ally."

"In that case," said Superman, "welcome to the team, Martian Manhunter!"

Martian Manhunter bowed. "I not only have a new planet . . . but a new family."

The Justice League congratulated their new friend.

"Let's party!" Cyborg hollered.

"Not so fast!" said a gruff voice. General Lane strode over. "I'm holding you all responsible for this damage."

Superman winked at Martian Manhunter. The Martian's eyes glowed, and General Lane's eyes blanked out.

The general danced like a robot, and Cy-bot rushed over and boogied with him. The Justice League laughed and cheered.